Captain Stormalong

Tale retold by Larry Dane Brimner
Illustrated by Chi Chung

Adviser: Dr. Alexa Sandmann, Professor of Literacy,
The University of Toledo; Member, International Reading Association

COMPASS POINT BOOKS
Minneapolis, Minnesota

Compass Point Books
3109 West 50th Street, #115
Minneapolis, MN 55410

Visit Compass Point Books on the Internet at *www.compasspointbooks.com*
or e-mail your request to *custserv@compasspointbooks.com*

Dedication
To George Frederick Brimner, a sailor's sailor and my dad.
 -LDB

Photograph ©: Bob Krist/Corbis, 28.

Editor: Catherine Neitge
Designer: Les Tranby

Library of Congress Cataloging-in-Publication Data
Brimner, Larry Dane.
   Captain Stormalong / tale retold by Larry Dane Brimner ; illustrated by Chi Chung.
      p. cm. — (The imagination series. Tall tales)
Summary: Describes some of the adventures of the legendary Captain Stormalong, who weighed some
four tons at the age of twelve and was known for riding a whale.
   ISBN 0-7565-0601-8 (hardcover)
   [1. Folklore—United States. 2. Stormalong, Albert Bulltop—Legends. 3. Tall tales.] I.
Chung, Chi, ill. II. Title. III. Series.
   PZ8.1.B757Cap 2004
   398.2—dc22   2003019299

Table of Contents

Off to Sea

Alfred Bulltop Stormalong— Stormy, for short—was the saltiest sailor who ever sailed the mighty seas. He was the biggest, too. Some folks will tell you he was sailing before oceans were invented or water vessels were crafted. That would be pretty near the truth, but not quite. The fact is that Stormy's great-great-great-great-great-great-great-great grandfather, or thereabouts, was chief architect on Noah's ark. That's near enough the beginning of oceans and vessels! Seawater flowed in Stormy's veins just as surely as blood flows in yours.

As a young lad way back in the first half of the 1800s, Stormy loved to watch ships come and go in the harbor. If truth is told, that's how he got his start at seafaring. The captain of the *Lady of the Sea* was trying to set sail for China out of Boston Harbor one morning and not having much luck at it. The ship's mate had not returned from town with a cabin boy, and everyone knows you can't set sail without one.

Just then, the mate's voice rang out from the dock. "Captain!" he called. "There's not a cabin boy in the whole of Boston, sir."

The news didn't put the captain in any kinder spirits. "Then you'll be my cabin boy!" he roared.

Stormy was standing but a stone's throw from the ship and couldn't help but overhear the captain's dilemma. He reached into his pocket and pulled out a note his mother had written, giving him permission to sign on with any ship that would have him. She'd written it after years of listening to Stormy plead with her to let him sail.

"Captain!" Stormy hollered, and raced down the dock. "I hear you're in need of a cabin boy, sir."

The captain looked toward the dock. There stood the biggest man he'd ever seen. He must have been 6 fathoms tall. He probably weighed 4 tons. "Aye," said the captain.

"Have you experience?"

"No, sir," Stormy said. "But I'm told the sea is in my veins."

The captain was thoughtful for a moment. Then he said, "Come aboard."

Stormy leapt from dock to deck in one catlike move. When he did, the ship pitched and then listed to one side. The captain clung to the wheel to keep from sliding into the brine.

"If you don't stand a little more to port, sir," the captain said, "you'll sink her before we can raise anchor."

"I'm sorry, sir," Stormy said. His face burned with embarrassment. He carefully placed one foot beside the port rail. When he did, the ship creaked and righted itself.

"That's better," said the captain. "Now tell me about yourself."

"Well, I'm 12, sir," Stormy said. "I have with me my mother's permission to sign on if you'll have me."

The captain couldn't believe what he'd heard. "Twelve, you say? Do you know anything about ships of this size?" he asked.

"I know she's a beauty," Stormy answered. Then looking around at the masts and rigging, he added, "But her lines are tangled." He reached out and untangled the snarl of ropes until each one fell into its proper place.

The captain liked that. He opened the ledger and extended his quill. "Sign on, lad," he said.

Stormy signed his name in the most grown-up way he could imagine. He wrote, "Stormalong, A. B."

The captain pondered Stormy's initials. "Able-Bodied, aye, lad?" asked the captain, smiling.

"Aye, captain," answered Stormy, who liked the sound of that much better than Alfred Bulltop. Ever since that day, sailors have written "A. B." after their names to indicate they're able-bodied seafarers.

"Raise anchor," ordered the captain.

The crew pulled and pulled at the winch, but it wouldn't budge. Something was wrong.

"With your permission, sir, I'll take a look," said Stormy.

"Be smart about it, lad," said the captain.

With a quick leap, Stormy was in the water. He soon saw the problem. The anchor was wedged under a huge rock.

Stormy pushed the rock aside and then swam to the surface. "Try her now!" he hollered.

This time, the winch turned like the hands of a well-oiled clock. Suddenly the *Lady of the Sea,* its sails unfurled, was drifting out to sea with the tide.

A Change of Course

Stormy loved the sea, but as his first ocean journey wore on, he knew something was missing. The young sailor thirsted for adventure. The only excitement aboard the *Lady of the Sea* was when it crossed the path of a hurricane, and that didn't happen often. Stormy got it into his head that the only place for adventure was aboard a spouter, as whaling ships were called.

The captain didn't want to lose a good sailor, but he agreed to put in a word for Stormy at their next port of call. "When you get all that excitement out of your system, lad," the captain said, "there'll always be a place for you on the *Lady of the Sea*." So with the captain's blessing, Stormy soon joined the crew of the *Gridiron.*

Life aboard a spouter was indeed exciting. The only thing predictable about chasing a whale was its unpredictability. You never knew just where a whale might lead you.

Take the time the captain of the *Gridiron* followed the whales up north. By then, Stormy was an incredibly strong young man who stood 10 fathoms tall. No one knew how he did it—least of all the whales—but he could harpoon four of the beasts at once by placing the irons carefully between his fingers and letting each one fly in a different direction. When news of Stormy's ability reached the colonies of whales, they made a beeline for the North Pole, to hide out under the ice. So the *Gridiron* followed.

Of all the lousy luck! Winter struck precisely at dawn the day after the *Gridiron* arrived in those northern waters. As quick as a mate can holler "Ahoy!" the water froze to a depth of 22 fathoms. The ship and all the men aboard her were stuck in the ice, and there they remained until the summer thaw.

Free at last, the crew decided on one last attempt at glory before charting a course back to Boston. They would try to find the great white whale—the one that sailors the world over spoke of with admiration and fear.

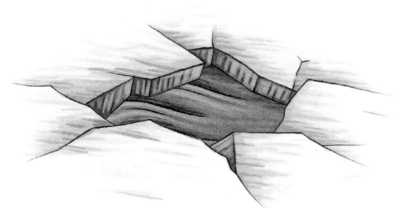

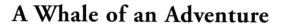

A Whale of an Adventure

The *Gridiron* was two months out of its frozen harbor when the mate in the crow's nest reported an uncharted island off the starboard rail. Just as the captain was about to name it, the island began to slide beneath the surface of the sea.

This wasn't an island at all. It was the great white whale, and it had been watching the *Gridiron* for some time. When it got too close for the whale's comfort, the King of the Deep slid beneath the surface of the sea. Then, as if to say, "Catch me if you can," it slapped its fluke down hard against the surface and sent a wave that tossed the *Gridiron* about like a toy.

The chase was on.

Stormy manned his station, harpoon at the ready. The whale had another trick up its flipper. It came up under the keel and rammed the boat. Everyone went flying, including Stormy. The whale turned and, as if grinning, looked right at Stormy and spat. The plume of water hit Stormy right in the eye!

"You!" Stormy roared, and he launched the harpoon.

The harpoon hit its mark. Whether the great whale was stunned or angry or a little of both, nobody could tell. It took off lickety-split, with Stormy holding the line. In the next moment, Stormy was jerked over the side and through the water. Hand over fist, Stormy pulled himself up the line until he sat astride the back of that whale. This only made the whale angrier, and thus began one of the greatest chases in all of seafaring history.

The whale zigged. It zagged. It rolled. It bucked.

Then, it dove. Stormy held tight. He rode that whale like a big-shot Western cowboy. Nothing would shake him loose.

He held tight until, at last, that whale's spirit was broken. Like a wild stallion that has been ridden until it accepts authority, the whale surfaced and waited for Stormy's direction.

"Giddyup, mate," Stormy said, in his best cowboy imitation, and he rode the whale back to the *Gridiron*.

Stormy Swallows the Anchor

After breaking the spirit of the King of the Deep, Stormy felt different about the sea. "Maybe it's time I did something else," he said to the captain one day.

"You're a born sailor," the captain said. "Aye, what else could you do?"

Stormy picked up an oar. It was the 18-footer he used as a tooth-pick. "Think I'll head west," Stormy said. "When I reach a place where no one knows what this water-slapper is, I'll try my hand at farming."

So it was that Stormy "swallowed the anchor." That's sailor talk for "he gave up the sea."

Stormy threw the oar over his shoulder and set off. After walking about 2,000 miles (3,200 kilometers), a stranger asked him what the odd contraption was that he had on his shoulder.

"That's the question I've been waiting to hear," said Stormy. "This is the place." He bought a farm and dug himself some potatoes.

By and by, Stormy became one of the most prosperous farmers in the region. Then a drought struck. Everywhere, farmers saw their crops wilt and wither. Their rich, black earth turned to dust and blew away, creating the Rocky Mountains when it settled. Only Stormy was spared.

He worked day and night. He worked so hard to save his crops that the sweat from his brow kept them watered, and the overflow created Utah's Great Salt Lake.

Then one day, Stormy looked around. There was a pleasant view of the new lake, but everyone knows a lake, no matter how salty, is not an ocean. Stormy sold his farm, threw his oar over his shoulder, and headed back east.

The Black Cliffs of Dover

When Stormy reached Boston, he knew he was home. The salt air stung his nostrils. The squawking gulls sounded like music to his ears. His heartbeat quickened, as did the pace with which he hastened to the wharf.

"Blow me down!" said Stormy. "Will you look at that?"

It was the biggest ship Stormy had ever seen.

"She's the *Courser,*" said a familiar voice.

It was his old friend, the captain of the *Lady of the Sea.* "Every sailor in these parts, and a few others, had a hand in making her. She's yours to command, lad, if you want her."

"If I want her!" Stormy had never heard anything more foolish. Of course he wanted her.

And what a ship she was! She carried a crew of 1,000 men. Her lifeboats had to have lifeboats. It was so far from bow to stern that the crew kept a stable of Arabian horses onboard to ride from one end of the ship to the other.

Stormy had years of narrow escapes aboard the *Courser,* but never so narrow as the time he had a shipload of soap to deliver to Holland. Everyone knows the shortest route to Holland is through the English Channel. Stormy wasn't worried about getting into the channel. What worried him was getting out. The passage along England's Black Cliffs of Dover was narrow, but he had a plan.

Two days before they reached Dover, he ordered his sailors to coat the sides of the *Courser* with soap. "Lay it on thick," he told them, and his sailors did. By the time they reached Dover, the ship was so slippery that even its paint slid off.

Stormy guided the ship into the passage. The ship creaked and groaned as it squeezed between the English cliffs and the coast of France. Stormy held the big wheel steady.

By slip and by slide, the big ship scraped through the passage. Of course, most of the soap on the port side was left behind. The Black Cliffs of Dover were now white with soap. Since that day, they have been called the White Cliffs of Dover.

As for Stormy, he delivered what was left of his cargo to Holland. A sailor, though, never stays in one port too long. There were other seas to sail, and Stormy wanted to sail them all.

The White Cliffs of Dover

England
Dover
English Channel
France

Captain Stormalong

Captain Stormalong first gained fame in an old sea chantey called "Old Stormalong." Sailors sang it as they worked to curb the boredom of life at sea. The different tales about this great seaman were collected by Frank Shay and published in his 1930 book, *Here's Audacity! American Legendary Heroes.*

Since then, the tales have been retold time and again, growing with each retelling. Each tale is a testament to the bravery of those souls, past and present, who sail the seas.

As for Stormy, it is said that he still commands the *Courser.* If you look skyward some night, you just might see him there among the stars. Folks say he pulls some of the mightiest catches ever right out of the Big Dipper!

Tuna Sandwiches

Alfred Bulltop Stormalong grew up on ostrich eggs (at least a dozen a day, scrambled) and clam chowder (20 barrels just for breakfast). After he became a sailor, he discovered other treats, like shark steaks and whale blubber soup. Since it's doubtful you will find whale blubber at your local grocery store, here's a recipe for tuna sandwiches that Stormy would have surely liked, too.

2 6-ounce cans solid white tuna, drained
2 hard-boiled eggs, chopped
3 stalks celery, chopped
$\frac{1}{2}$ cup mayonnaise
1 teaspoon yellow mustard

$\frac{1}{2}$ teaspoon dried basil leaves, crushed
$\frac{1}{4}$ teaspoon black pepper, or to taste
4 potato or kaiser rolls, split
1 tomato, sliced thinly
4 leaves lettuce

Combine the first seven ingredients in a bowl, folding together until well mixed. Cover and chill for an hour or longer. When ready to serve, spoon the tuna mixture onto the bottom half of each roll. Top with lettuce leaves and/or tomato slices. Then cover with the other half of the roll. Serves four sailors.

Glossary

architect—a person who designs structures

astride—with a leg on each side

bow—the very front of a ship

brine—salt water, or the sea

chantey—a sailor's work song

crow's nest—platform near the top of a ship's mast

dilemma—problem

drought—a long spell of very dry weather

fathom—a unit of measurement, used especially to measure the depth of water; a fathom is equal to 6 feet (1.83 meters)

fluke—a triangle-shaped half of a whale's tail

irons—harpoons

keel—the wooden or metal piece that runs along the bottom of a boat

ledger—a ship's log or record book

listed—leaned to one side

port—the left side of a ship looking forward

port of call—a place where ships dock for supplies, repairs, or cargo

predictable—known in advance; expected

seafaring—the business of being a sailor

starboard—the right side of a ship looking forward

stern—the back end of a ship

Did You Know?

➤ The largest animals on Earth are blue whales. They can be 110 feet (33 meters) long and weigh as much as 200 tons. In fact, they are the largest creatures to EVER live on Earth.

Want to Know More?

At the Library

Metaxas, Eric. *Stormalong: The Legendary Sea Captain.* New York: Rabbit Ears Books, 1995.

Osborne, Mary Pope. *American Tall Tales.* New York: Alfred A. Knopf, 1991.

Stoutenburg, Adrien. *American Tall Tales.* New York: Puffin Books, 1976.

Walker, Paul Robert. *Big Men, Big Country.* San Diego: Harcourt Paperbacks, 2000.

On the Web

For more information on *Captain Stormalong,* use FactHound to track down Web sites related to this book.

1. Go to *www.compasspointbooks.com/ facthound*
2. Type in this book ID: 0756506018
3. Click on the *Fetch It* button.

Your trusty FactHound will fetch the best Web sites for you!

Through the Mail

Whale Conservation Institute

191 Weston Road
Lincoln, MA 01773
800/969-4253
question@oceanalliance.org
To obtain information on this organization that works to protect whales and their ocean environment through research and education

On the Road

New Bedford Whaling Museum

18 Johnny Cake Hill
New Bedford, MA 02740-6398
508/997-0046
To explore the history of whaling around the world

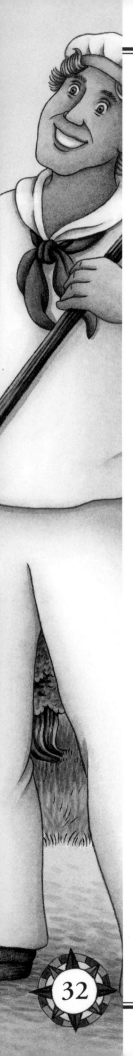

Index

About the Author

Larry Dane Brimner has written more than 100 books for young people, including the award-winning *Merry Christmas, Old Armadillo* (Boyds Mills Press) and *The Littlest Wolf* (HarperCollins Publishers). He is also the reteller of several other Tall Tales, including *Calamity Jane, Casey Jones, Davy Crockett,* and *Molly Pitcher.* Larry "swallowed the anchor" long ago and now resides in landlocked Tucson, Arizona.

About the Illustrator

Chi Chung was born in Taipei, Taiwan, and received her master's degree from California State University in Los Angeles. She has always loved to draw and paint. She lives in New York City.